W9-CGW-756

Written by Stephanie Spence
Illustrated by Gladys Jose

All rights reserved. No part of this publication may be reproduced, stored in a retrieval system, or transmitted in any form or by any means-electronic, mechanical, photocopying, recording, or otherwise-without written permission of Tangerine Press.

Copyright © 2016 Scholastic Inc.

an imprint of
SCHOLASTIC
www.scholastic.com

Scholastic, Tangerine Press, and associated logos are trademarks and/or registered trade-marks of Scholastic Inc.

Published by Tangerine Press, an imprint of Scholastic Inc.
557 Broadway
New York, NY 10012

10 9 8 7 6 5 4 3 2 1

ISBN: 978-1-338-03830-9

Printed in Jiaxing, China   506664 06/16

Winter's Song

By Stephanie Spence

Illustrated by Gladys Jose

Among the folded valleys and sleepy pines of Snowfall,
every villager—from the biggest frostbear to the smallest snowboy—
awaits the winter solstice, the shortest day and longest night of the year.

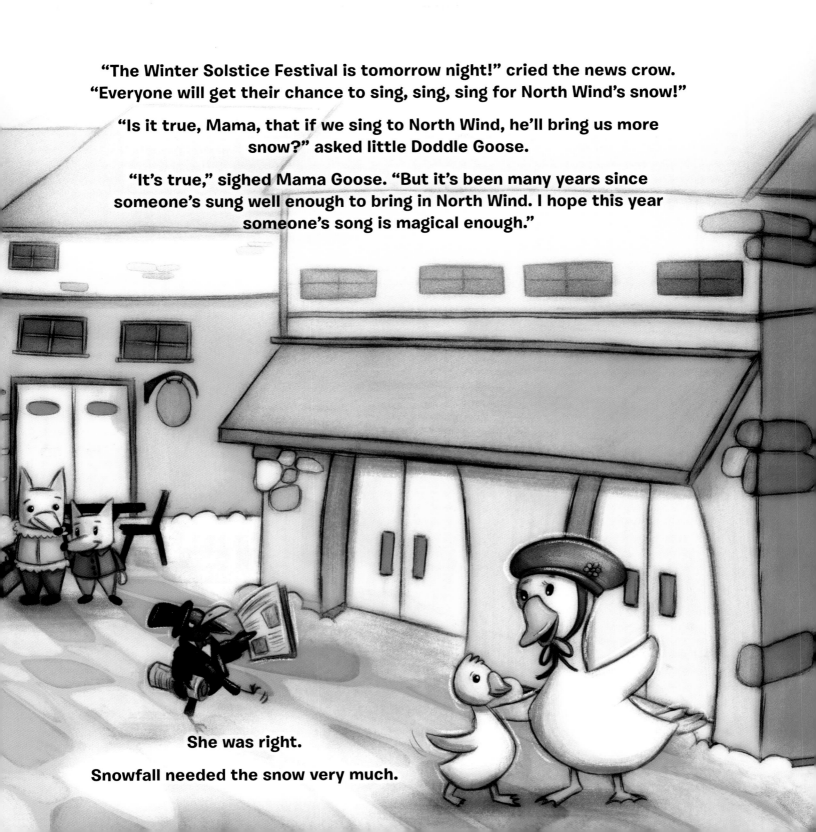

"The Winter Solstice Festival is tomorrow night!" cried the news crow. "Everyone will get their chance to sing, sing, sing for North Wind's snow!"

"Is it true, Mama, that if we sing to North Wind, he'll bring us more snow?" asked little Doddle Goose.

"It's true," sighed Mama Goose. "But it's been many years since someone's sung well enough to bring in North Wind. I hope this year someone's song is magical enough."

She was right.

Snowfall needed the snow very much.

Two of Snowfall's hopeful singers were snowgirl Pearl and her brother Puff.
They hopped toward the schoolhouse, practicing their songs.

"My baritone is the best," Puff bragged to his sister.
"I'm sure to be prince of this year's festival."

"Oh, brother. You have a voice like a frog's!" said Pearl.

"But my soprano is snowriffic," she gloated.
"I'm positive I'll be princess."
"Your voice is even squeakier than a snowmouse's!" said Puff.

"Hmph!" said Pearl. "We'll see whose voice is best. It's almost my turn!"

Mrs. Chilton, the music teacher, raised her palm.
"Ready, Pearl? One, and a two, and—"

Kkkkrrrrt!
Her shriek shattered the icicles outside the window.

The whole class laughed.
Brittle, the loudest of them all, laughed
so hard her bow almost fell off. Her best friend
Berg tapped Pearl on the shoulder. "We'll be sure to
call you if we need our windows de-iced!"

Puff and Pearl almost
MELTED from
EMBARRASSMENT.

"QUIET!"
huffed Mrs. Chilton. "I expect you all to practice your festival songs. I'll see you all in the square tomorrow evening at six o'clock sharp."

The class tumbled out.

"I feel terrible," moaned Puff.

"I'm sorry I made fun of you," said Pearl.

Brittle and Berg blazed by and sang, "Puff and Pearl, Pearl and Puff.
Pearl's all squawk and Puff's too gruff."

"North Wind will never bring us snow if it's left up to you two," teased Berg.

"Yeah, what were those notes again?" Brittle joined in.

"AaaaaaAAAAAAAAAAA!
And
OOOOOOOOOOOO–uh oh,"

Berg and Brittle
bellowed and laughed.

Pearl and Puff had had enough.
"LEAVE US ALONE!" They shouted.
Then all at once, they sang out one big note
and their voices blended beautifully.

Everyone was amazed, even Pearl and Puff.
"You know, your voice is so low," said Pearl.
"Why, your voice is so high," said Puff.

"But maybe if we sing together our voices might sound
good enough to bring North Wind and his snow!"

Winter solstice finally arrived. Snowfall was decorated in tinsel and the villagers were enjoying the festival.

"Come get your sweet crumbly cakes," Mr. Lump called to passersby.

Though everyone was enjoying the festival, they all knew the town was slowly melting.

Snowfall needed North Wind to come!

Mayor Snowbell, dressed in her finest velvet robes, flew to the stage to announce the long-awaited event. "Greetings, citizens of Snowfall," she began. "It is my honor to welcome you to our annual Winter Solstice Festival. Let the concert begin!"

Brittle was the first snowgirl to sing. Snowflakes swirled as caribou bounced behind her. She rocked and rolled her version of "Winter's Song," hitting every note. But North Wind did not come.

Berg was up next.
As he played his violin, swans dipped and
swayed and played the icicle chimes.
But still North Wind did not come.

One by one, singers and musicians performed their renditions of "Winter's Song."
They jazzed and jammed and jumped and sang, but North Wind still did not come.

"Oh, my! If North Wind doesn't come this year, Snowfall will melt into Waterfall," said Mayor Snowbell. "Isn't there anyone left whose song will welcome North Wind?"

From far in the back of the crowd, two small hands went up. It was Pearl and Puff.

"Oh, yes, Pearl and Puff. Come to the stage, children."

Brother and sister climbed up what seemed like a thousand steps.

Puff's first note was too low. Pearl's first note was too high.

Someone snickered in the crowd, but the
two little snowballs held their heads up.
"May we start again?" they asked.
"Of course," said the mayor.

Puff and Pearl held hands and started again.
This time, it was magic.
The audience began to sing along with them.

"WINTER'S SONG"
(Sung to the tune of "Twinkle, Twinkle Little Star")

Freeze and frost, snow and sleet,
Take away the summer's heat.

Chilly wind to bare the trees,
Scarves and stockings to the knees.

Let's link arms and sing along;
Together we sing "Winter's Song."

Suddenly, a rumble rose
from behind the mountains.
It was North Wind riding in
on clouds of frost and snow!

"Never, in all my ages, have I heard such a duet!" North Wind declared. "Your voices were filled with the sparkle, magic, and harmony this town needed."

Suddenly, a rainbow of light twisted in the sky. A woman in a glowing gown floated down and sat next to North Wind. Everyone gasped—Aurora, North Wind's sister, had come too!

"No one has sung "Winter's Song" magically enough to bring us both," said Aurora, smiling at Puff and Pearl. "Come, brother, let's make this a winter for the ages!"

North Wind blew a mighty cold wind. His breath fattened up the puffy snow hills and polished the icy roads.

Aurora put her hands into the sky and arranged the stars to shine brighter than ever. Then she covered the town with a sparkling blanket of white snow.

Aurora and North Wind began to sing.
North Wind low, Aurora high. Puff and Pearl joined in too.

That night, every villager—from the wildest wolf to the
smallest snowmouse—joined hands and sang along to
"Winter's Song."